Hey, kids!
See if you can spot Santa,
Mrs Claus and Reindeer
hidden throughout
the story.

To..
You made it onto Santa's NICE list – WELL DONE!

MERRY CHRISTMAS!

Love from...

I SAW SANTA IN WALES

Written by JD Green

Illustrated by Nadja Sarell and Srimalie Bassani

Hometown World

Santa's not planned his holiday this year.
Mrs Claus says, "Shall we go to Wales then, my dear?
You've told us how it is your favourite place,
but remember, the children should not see your face."

"Yes, Wales!" says Santa. "That's the best place of all!
Great sights, tasty bites, super shops, big and small."

Mrs Claus says, "Let's pack. We can head off tonight!
Remember what I said? You must keep out of sight!"

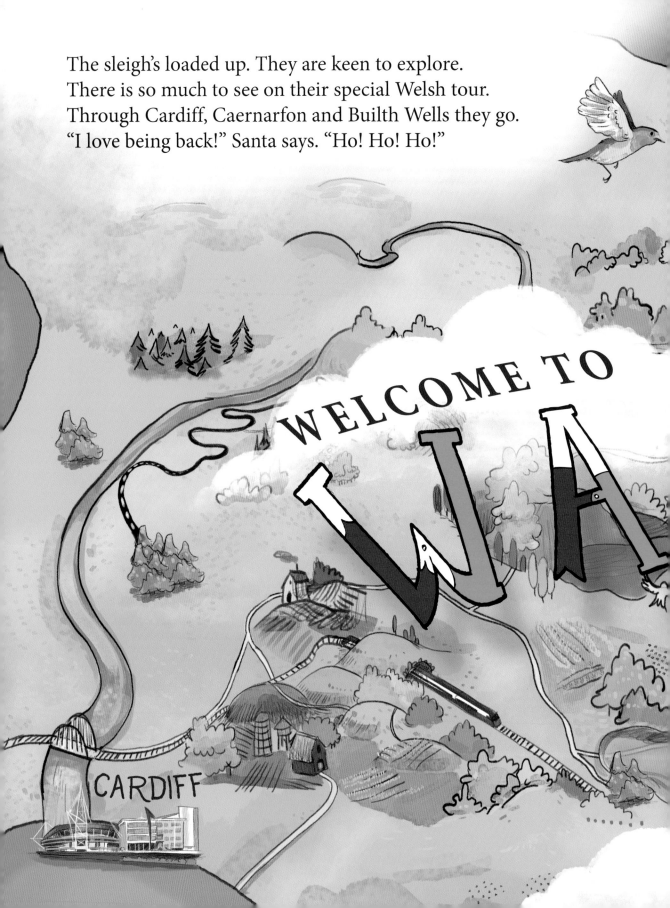

The sleigh's loaded up. They are keen to explore.
There is so much to see on their special Welsh tour.
Through Cardiff, Caernarfon and Builth Wells they go.
"I love being back!" Santa says. "Ho! Ho! Ho!"

WELCOME TO WA

CARDIFF

It's a family tradition, when they go away,
to buy a few gifts to remember their stay.

So smart Mrs Claus came prepared with a list,
she knows what to buy, and no friend will be missed.

Santa thinks buying nice gifts is quite tough.
He's feeling confused – there's just so much stuff!

His baskets soon fill up with goodies galore,
such as Welsh cakes, oysters, pasties and more.

Reindeer is dressed in a clever disguise,
so he will not be spotted by keen little eyes.

He's ready to sightsee and have lots of fun,
visiting each cool new place, one by one.

The Clauses are done buying gifts for their friends,
it's time for sightseeing before the trip ends.

But at the North Pole, Head Elf checks the mail.
He opens one letter and turns very pale…

Dear Santa,

I want to be a zookeeper when I grow up.
I would love a furry lion onesie for Christmas.

Please.

Love, Noah xxx
Age 5
from Rhyl

P.S. Did I see you at the Welsh Mountain Zoo?
There was a guy with a big, white beard eating
an ice cream in the giraffe lookout!
Was it you?

Dear Santa,

My favourite place in the whole wide world is the ocean! Please can I have a snorkel and flippers for Christmas? Thank you!

By the way, I was at LC Swansea yesterday. I didn't have my glasses on while I was swimming, but I saw someone with a big, white beard and a red-and-white bathing suit. Was it you? Please write back and tell me.

Love, Emma
Age 7
from Llanelli

At home in the North, Head Elf says, "This won't do! One sighting is terrible – now we've had two!"

Santa should really be taking more care,
it seems more children have spotted him there.

Dear Santa,

I would love, love, love a big, pink unicorn!
I drew one for you here.

Love, Bella x X x

Age 5¾
from Port Talbot

P.S. Did I see you at Afan Forest Park,
wearing green hiking boots and a red-and-
white striped backpack? It even sounded like
you were whistling 'We'll keep a welcome in
the hillside'. Am I right?

AFAN
FOREST
PARK

Reading the mail, Head Elf shakes his head.
This letter has caused him to turn rather red!

Hey Santa!

Was that you at Caernarfon Castle? I was
there with my best friend, Bobby. I know you
live in the North Pole, but it really looked just
like you sitting on a bench, wearing sunglasses
and drinking a milkshake. Oh, and we would
like new cricket bats for Christmas, please!

Bye!

William
Age 7
from Wrexham

In Lapland, Head Elf can't believe what he's seeing,
another *two* children have seen Santa fleeing!

Hello Santa,

My name is Olivia and I am 6½.
I like horse riding and would like new
boots for Christmas.

I went to the Royal Welsh Show. Did you go,
too? I'm pretty sure I saw you riding a horse
and eating a hot dog!

Was that really you?

Love, Olivia
from Merthyr Tydfil

HOT

NO SLEIGHS ALLOWED

BOATING LAKE PARK

Hi Santa,

I am 8 and I would like a real duck this Christmas. My grandpa and I were watching the ducks at Boating Lake Park, Cwmbran, when we saw a big, red sleigh on the other side of the pond. I heard the park keeper say sleighs are not allowed.

Was that you?

James
from Newport

The holiday's over; the shopping is done.
Wales was brilliant – they had so much fun!

Now they are home, Head Elf lets Santa know,
he's been spotted in Wales several times now. Oh, no!

Noah, age 5

Dear Noah,
Yes, you did spot me at the Welsh Mountain Zoo! I was on my summer holiday in Wales. Enjoy your lion suit.

Love, Santa x

Emma, age 7

Dear Emma,
Yes, you did spot me at the pool! Wales is my favourite place to visit. Have fun with your snorkel and flippers.

Love, Santa x

Bella, age 5¾

Dear Bella,
Yes, you did spot me at the forest park! I was on my summer holiday in Wales. Have fun with your pink unicorn!

Love, Santa x

Mrs Claus says to Santa, "I know what to do.
We can make this all good with a letter or two."

When Christmas arrives, all the children who wrote
get one extra gift, and inside is a note…

Hello little one,

On my summer break, I like getting away,
so I go to Wales, the best place to stay.
There's so much in Wales that I like to see,
there's really no place that I'd rather be.

So keep a lookout, 'cause you never know,
if I might be somewhere that you like to go.
And if you can find time I like nothing better,
than hearing from you, so write me a letter!

Merry Christmas!
Love,
Santa

XXX

Written by JD Green
Illustrated by Nadja Sarell and Srimalie Bassani
Additional art by Jerry Pyke and Darran Holmes
Designed by Geff Newland

First published by HOMETOWN WORLD in 2018
Hometown World Ltd
7 Northumberland Buildings
Bath
BA1 2JB

www.hometownworld.co.uk

Follow us @hometownworldbooks

Hey, kids! Flick back and see if you can spot Santa, Mrs Claus and Reindeer hidden throughout the story.